Words to Know Before You Read

everyone

kickball

now

play

run

sport

team

turns

www.rourkeeducationalmedia.com

Edited by Precious McKenzie
Illustrated by Anita DuFalla
Art Direction and Page Layout by Renee Brady

Dedication: To Johnny for supporting me in everything! –Sam

Library of Congress PCN Data

It's My Turn / Sam Williams
ISBN 978-1-61810-163-1 (hard cover) (alk. paper)
ISBN 978-1-61810-296-6 (soft cover)
Library of Congress Control Number: 2012936764

Rourke Educational Media
Printed in the United States of America,
North Mankato, Minnesota

rourkeeducationalmedia.com

customerservice@rourkeeducationalmedia.com • PO Box 643328 Vero Beach, Florida 32964

It's My Turn

By Sam Williams

Illustrated by Anita DuFalla

"Hey, everyone!"

4

"Let's play!"

5

"I'm on your team."

6

"Can I play?"

8

"I'm kicking the ball first."

"It's my turn again.
I scored a home run."

13

"No, it's not your turn. It's Abby's turn."

14

15

"Hey! It's my turn!"

16

"That's not taking turns."

"I'm not going to play kickball with you if you don't take turns!"

"It's O.K."

After Reading Activities

You and the Story...

What does being a good sport mean?

Who was not being a good sport?

What did he do?

What do you do to be a good sport?

Words You Know Now...

Can you find two words that start and end with the same letter?
What two words start with the same sound?

everyone	run
kickball	sport
now	team
play	turns

You Could...Start Your Own Game with Friends

- Who will play on your teams?

- Invite everyone that you want to play.

- Decide together what game you will play.

- Decide what rules you will use in playing your game.

- Go play your game with your friends...remember to take turns!

About the Author

Sam lives with his two dogs, Abby and Cooper, in Florida. Abby and Cooper play together every day...in between naps.

Ask The Author!
www.rem4students.com

About the Illustrator

Acclaimed for its versatility in style, Anita DuFalla's work has appeared in many educational books, newspaper articles, and business advertisements and on numerous posters, book and magazine covers, and even giftwraps. Anita's passion for pattern is evident in both her artwork and her collection of 400 patterned tights. She lives in the Friendship neighborhood of Pittsburgh, Pennsylvania with her son, Lucas.